RED MOUNTAIN CUT

And Other Short Reads from the Natural City

stories by

Steve Brammell

Finishing Line Press
Georgetown, Kentucky

RED MOUNTAIN CUT

And Other Short Reads from the Natural City

ACKNOWLEDGMENTS

Earlier versions of these stories were published regularly in *Birmingham
Magazine* as "The Natural City". Thanks to editor Joe O'Donnell for the
opportunity. "Southern Snow" and "Honey" appeared in *The Tiny Seed
Literary Journal.* "Fourth of July" appeared in *The Dead Mule School of
Southern Literature.* "Mine" appeared in *the Toho Journal.*

Publisher: Leah Huete de Maines
Editor: Christen Kincaid
Cover Art: Bakr Magrabi
Author Photo: Tony Valainis
Cover Design: Elizabeth Maines McCleavy

Order online: www.finishinglinepress.com
also available on amazon.com

Author inquiries and mail orders:
Finishing Line Press
P. O. Box 1626
Georgetown, Kentucky 40324
U. S. A.

Table of Contents

BAMBOO

for T.K.

He saws until the teeth bite open air. The big bamboo falls gently through its neighbors with the sound of wind. He carries his son in a sling strapped to his chest, a yard-long piece of cane under his arm. Coming out of the grove the baby's eyes widen and blink as they move back and forth between sky and his face.

As he cuts the notch where his lips will go, he thinks of the uncle who always reeked of beer, the one the family blamed on 'The War'. The summer he turned ten that uncle came home briefly from the VA smelling sweet and clean with aftershave and Lifebuoy soap, a kind man when sober, a man with the deep vein of melancholy.

Drunk, his uncle gloried in the war he'd seen, the Pacific Ocean bright with fire, a hundred guns blasting, kamikazes falling from the sky like avenging angels. But now his uncle sat on the front porch nodding to the neighbors, whittling down sticks until nothing remained.

One day, he walked past the porch with a cane pole, on his way to the creek. "Go cut me the end off your pole," his uncle told him.

Coming back with a string of catfish he saw his uncle waiting on the step, a flute made from cane in his hand. He watched his uncle raise the flute to his lips and wait with his eyes closed, as though listening for something he could not yet hear. Then a note came out, a long note so sad and lonely floating over the yard, a note that opened up a space inside him like the cooing of a mourning dove or the sound of his mother crying.

"A woman taught me how to play," was all his uncle said. "A woman from Japan."

He puts his own cane in the vice and drills four holes on top and one underneath for his thumb. He, too, went off to war in the Orient. One day in a market in Saigon he came upon an old man selling bamboo flutes and bought one, thinking of his sad uncle who had soon gone back to the bottle.

He had no woman to teach him notes, but the air in Vietnam was filled with music. This flute had a deeper voice than the one his uncle carved. The notes it made sank from their own weight to pool like darkness in the low places. He practiced every night sailing up the Mekong. Once the notes he played lured a tiger, the beautiful beast haunting him from the bank with its cold burning eyes. The next day his best friend died in an ambush.

This flute he's made is large, its bamboo thick with so much space to fill with breath. He takes it from the garage to the basement with his son cradled in a carrier. Before he brings it to his lips, he lets his life since the war sing to him—the broken marriages, the drinking and the drugs. He lets the silence of the monks in the Carolina mountains who saved his life flow through him, and he thinks of the sound his young wife makes as she sleeps.

Now, above his son, his very first child, he begins to play.

SWIMMING LESSONS

Through bare feet he can feel the water lap the hull. He unties the lines, throws them on the dock, backs away from his slip through a lazy cloud of exhaust. Out on the smoothness of the bay he gives the engines gas, raising up a rooster tail of spray, turning wide to starboard where the channel opens to the Gulf.

The sun is rising over Florida as he calls and leaves a message at the office to cancel all his meetings. Everybody said he'd need more time, but he didn't know what they meant until last night. He had to let himself go down without a fight, let death rob the air from his lungs, fill him with its weight, slam him hard against the bottom.

He had left Birmingham at midnight and set the cruise control on eighty, playing Ravel and Debussy as he flew down I-65. The urn sat on the seat beside him. "Bring me the album in the top dresser drawer," she told him last week from her hospital bed. Those old color photos had leached to amber scenes of a very young woman and a little boy, each one with the ocean shining in the background pulling at his memory's eye. "Those were the best times of my life," she whispered, a new machine plugged into her side. "Just the two of us and the sun and the sea. You and I could swim like porpoises." She was a knockout then, a diver's body in a two piece and turban, wearing movie-star shades.

The towers on the beach glow like marble in the morning light. He heads straight out at full throttle until he can see no land. He cuts the engines. The silent boat rises on a gentle swell. Grief rolls over him again, the biggest wave of all. Curled on the bed in the bow cabin, over and over he nearly drowns, breaking through the surface of his agony, eyes stinging, gasping for air. "Remember, you promised you wouldn't put me in the ground." She had motioned for him to bend down close to her face. He smelled something strange on her breath.

He pries the bronze lid off with a key. Her ashes pour like salt. He cannot bring himself to watch her go and turns his head. When he feels the urn is empty, he lets it drop with a hollow splash. He fixes a drink.

He isn't sure how long he sleeps. Thunderheads obscure the whole western sky. He makes it in right before the storm, the palm trees around the marina in a frenzy, the rain drenching him on the way to his car. "It was our first time and you had just learned how to walk." She always giggled when she told her favorite story. "I put you down and got distracted, fiddling with my blanket. When I turned around you were already in the water, staring at that

3

breaker about to hit you."

The sunset is beautiful after the storm but he stays inside the house, looking at the beach with the whitest sand in the world.

FANDANGO

The TV weatherman shows a Doppler leviathan, flashing and fiery as it swallows Tuscaloosa County whole. On the deck he watches black wall clouds approaching, a half million dollars' worth of house behind him, a castle built of playing cards and glue. Wind and rain arrive in waves then turn to hail the size of golf balls. He tries to keep his focus amid the crescendo, the desk reverberating beneath his hand, all the windows fogging from the sudden cold.

He's nearly finished with a piece he's been working on for weeks. Composed in those interludes he steals from his business, his marriage, and even his children, the notes arrange themselves when and where they want, coming from a source beyond his ear, moving the pencil up and down the lines.

Today he doesn't go to church with his family, locked in the crow's nest room he added to the architect's plans. Surrounded by shelves of recorded music, by keyboards and guitars, he listens to nothing but the rage of barometric pressure and dissipating heat, atmosphere brought to a boiling point by the war of seasons. Down in that cellar thirty years ago he knelt beside his mother and prayed while his father squinted through a crack in the foundation, hoping for a glimpse of what made the growing jet plane roar. Spared their lives but not their home, or store, or town, he would never forget the sound of Armageddon.

He writes another chord to be strummed as hard as fear. He sees of himself in Spain at 21, sneaking down to stare into the face of the bull just before it charged into the ring. His junior year abroad he studied with a master in Seville, a classical genius who learned to play flamenco from Andalusian gypsies.

The hail stops suddenly, making way for that stillness through which tornadoes move. He lays his pencil down, wipes the window clear to view the sky, low and ragged, tinged with green.

Across the trees in Alabaster the siren begins to wail its single note, announcing the end of the world. He strains to hear what terrifies him more than death, hear it coming the way it's always described—louder than a freight train, the engine noise of chaos.

But though he knows he should be running for the basement, he sits back down and fills the lines with music—matador and bull at the end of their bloody dance, the air wild with cheers and roses, rapturous women spinning around a fire with castanets, finishing his fandango.

THE POTTER'S TOAST

We drive to the clay pit one November afternoon. She talks of time before metal, how the universe could rest inside a perfect bowl. I shovel Alabama clay the color of dawn into cold, heavy buckets. Up on top, she takes a lump and rolls it long and ropy between her hands "to see if it wants to be worked". She wraps the clay around her wrist like a pagan bracelet.

A potter's home smells of earth and fire. I ask to see the kiln. She tells me I must wait.

Resting on her knees in my truck, her hands had looked old and weakened by too much effort. Now, as she sits on her stool, those hands cut and knead and slap, dipping water to bless both clay and wheel.

"I'd like you to hold this for a moment," she says. The mass of clay feels warm as flesh.

She trips a switch. Clay and wheel turn into a blur. "I've never told anyone this," she confides, "but I'm always afraid to touch it the first time, as though I'm about to do something terribly wrong." Her hands hover like the gypsy's above a crystal ball.

She bows, closes her eyes, presses down with gentle force, a mother's hands on the head of a jumpy child. Molten lava leaks between her fingers. A muscle trembles in her jaw. She mumbles something.

"My father was an old-style missionary," she tells me. "And I was always such a physical girl. I made the poor man suffer so."

Her hands come away from a perfect mound, Aphrodite's breast. She feeds more water to the clay. "Now watch," she says, and with her thumb opens up a well.

She asks me about myself as she works. I can't keep my eyes from the spinning, changing clay that seems to take its pleasure from what secrets her fingers speak. She listens as I tell her everything.

When the bowl is finished, she leaves it on the wheel and leads me to the back where she shows me all her many glazes, the alchemy jars she employs to change plain mud into precious stone. The kiln stands in yet another room. "It's cooled enough to open now," she says as we go in.

She pulls the handle. The air smells of ashes. She removes a goblet blue enough and deep enough to hold the whole evening sky and puts it firmly in my hand.

SOUTHERN SNOW

His daughter is too young to remember the last time the sky fell. From this hill on Highland golf course they can see Birmingham's abandoned downtown towers and hear the freeway's Niagara rush to get everybody home. He watches the clouds take on a peculiar cast, as though they are spun of wool instead of vapor. The plunging temperature thrills him. He just prays the future isn't made of ice.

Only yesterday he had shown his daughter the small white blossoms of winter honeysuckle, held her up to inhale that January perfume as he whispered its name in her ear. Now she is bundled in goose down against an Arctic Alabama wind and the word he must teach her stays high overhead, flickering on a radar beam.

While grownups plunder supermarket shelves of potato chips and milk, children gather by the window keeping watch for another world. His older son has already sailed on gravity once before, that day two years ago when the golf course became a roller coaster ride. Three crows glide above the Piggly Wiggly store. He hears them calling for the miracle to begin.

At first it looks like smoke. The hard-edged city skyline starts to waver and fade, an illusion all along, a dream with the meter running—he sees a veil dropped by a magician make it vanish. Block by block, visibility draws to a close.

He's read that every flake must form around a nucleus, bits of Sahara Desert dust, particles of Mount St. Helens still traveling the stratosphere, dead stars pulverized by time. He takes his daughter in his arms. He yearns for her to learn all there is to know.

She screams with joy. The flakes are enormous and wet, coming straight down, spinning like whirligigs, sticking to the grass like dandelion fluff. Traffic slides to a halt on Clairmont Avenue. A runner twirls with his arms out.

He waits until the ground is gone then puts his daughter down to take her first steps on virgin territory. He licks the sweet cold feathery dew from his lips. The white curtain descends around them. Together, lost without a care, he knows the time is right to teach her the word for snow.

JAZZ

Every day he gets up at sunrise and walks the morning, a wooden staff his only company. Sometimes he roams Forest Park and Southside, other days Mountain Brook and Homewood or the long crest of Red Mountain. Once or twice a week he drives somewhere, city or country, never planning a route, never with a watch, guided only by his curiosity.

The carriage house has been a home to all his grown-up children, summers and semesters off, two breakups, one divorce and a trial with the artist's life. That last experiment left him with a downstairs studio, good light, and brick wall exposed. Another wall he knocked down himself, putting in a spiral staircase to the upstairs apartment where he keeps his books, a cot for the nights he stays up late, and his golden alto sax.

In the big house across the lawn, his wife and daughters prepare Thanksgiving dinner. He listens to the rain, remembers this morning when he hiked through the downpour in his new waterproof suit, his favorite streets and alleys transformed to rushing streams, amazed how the scintillating fabric enfolded every house and tree and car, turning them all to precious gifts.

The plaque his company gave him hangs above the old coal fireplace. His dictionary tells him the word retire means to withdraw or move away. For a month he dreamed he was lost in a cave. He slides his hand across his thigh, muscled again like the legs of that high school boy who ran the mile. After the meeting, his boss—a good man with an axe put in his hand—came to his office and told him he was still young enough to start another life. He listens to the rain and wonders how anyone can know if the blind-side punch will bring them to their knees or to their senses.

His youngest son, the sculptor, left behind a wealth of cabinets, shelves and a workbench along one wall. He had tried to appreciate the art his son produced, weird conglomerations of electrical circuitry, rusted junk, and heat-molded plastic. "My use of castoff objects represents the alienation I feel from this consumer society," the boy explained.

Perhaps his son, gone away to Oregon, might understand these things now lining the shelves and filling the cabinets—the rocks that catch his eye a thousand different ways, the nuts and acorns and seedpods, the birds' eggs and insect shells, the whole drawer filled with cocoons. And why had he never been to a yard sale until this summer? What treasures he found: books on every subject, tools to dissect and carve, even equipment from a college lab—a microscope that lets him see what swims in a drop of birdbath scum. The rain begins to come down hard again and he wants to light a fire but he must wait.

The big house fills with people. His wife holds court, laughing with the grandchildren, serving up dessert, refilling everybody's drinks. Her own career has taken off in the last five years, and it sometimes seems her smart phone rules her life. "How are you doing?" she asks him in the kitchen as he does the dishes, and he wants to tell her all the secrets about himself he has learned, wants to take her into the rain. "I'll be in Atlanta tomorrow through Saturday," she says.

Out in the carriage house he uses a chisel to break up blocks of Walker County coal for the fireplace. Later, as he watches these black stones burn with the light of the morning sun, he climbs the spiral staircase for the brand-new saxophone he doesn't yet know how to play.

REUNION

His aunts surround Rebecca, asking about her family. They compliment her on her manners, how pretty she is, and her taste in clothes. He has prepared her for weeks for her first trip to the South, but now he realizes his fears have nothing to do with this brave fine woman he is about to marry.

"Have you been up to visit the homeplace yet?" old uncle Henry asks him over a table piled with family recipes. Outside the sun burns white in all that glass. Cars line both sides of the road for a quarter mile, spilling over from the parking lot of the VFW Hall. He feels queasy in the heat, gorged on squash casserole and smoked wild turkey. Two distant cousins, whose names he can't remember, play horseshoes in the shade beneath a willow oak. He nods to them as he heads across a pasture dotted with fire ant mounds, wondering why some families wither away, while others can't help but thrive.

Up the hill, the whine of cicadas nearly hypnotizes him. His father once took him to a grove of cottonwoods in Illinois and showed him the litter of dead and dying insects with cellophane wings and bodies made of gold and jade. "How would you like to wait seventeen years underground, live only for a week or two, and end up like this?"

Raised a mill rat's son in Ensley, his father had joined the Air Force straight out of high school, luring his mother down from these hills with promises of seeing the great wide world. No matter where they lived, his mother kept her Mason jar of rocky dirt scooped from this place on the day she left.

He can't remember all the times his father came home drunk, all the fights, the blows that spun his mother through the air in terror's slow motion as though she were dancer. When his father broke the jar, storming out into the damp German night, he got a spoon and collected her precious soil, glinting with shards of glass, from the kitchen floor.

At the top of the hill the house is gone, burned down by vandals ten years before, but the tall chimney still stands, proud as a Roman tower. Uncle Henry keeps the grass cut as best he can, pulling a Bush Hog through once a month on his way to tend the cemetery. Lately there must have been plenty of rain because the homeplace is ablaze with dandelions.

He sits on a corner of the stone foundation and looks over the valley and tries again to decide if he will invite his father to the wedding. Rebecca has helped him with his anger but he knows he has just begun to tap its black root to drain the poison. At his feet a large dandelion has turned round and white, and he picks it, aware that he has never really looked at one before. He studies that delicate outer sphere through which he can see a dark, compact core and thinks of a summer many years before—his mother packing her bags, his young father kneeling on the grass, gathering his bouquet, blowing dry dandelions into clouds of tiny parachutes, each one dangling a sharp ebony seed.

ABLAZE

The stallion's head is level with his own, the neck stretched over the side of the stall, a horse eye staring at him. "Meet Butterfly," his daughter says. "Isn't he the most beautiful thing you've ever seen?"

He reaches out halfway, afraid the animal might bite him, then he runs his finger up a long, veined cheek as soft as an expensive glove. That massive body shudders and stamps a hoof.

"I'm the only one who can ride him," his daughter says, taking down the bridle with its silver bit. She's even more stunning than her mother—taller, with a more athletic build, her features graced by another degree of perfection.

"You need to get through to her," his ex-wife sighed when she met him at the airport. On his way back to Mexico to negotiate for Aztec treasures, he scheduled a last-minute stop in Birmingham.

He thinks how somber his daughter seems now that puberty is finished with her. The funny little girl who used to memorize every joke she heard, who waited for him to get home from the museum to try them out—every inflection, every accent done just right—that same endearing child has turned into this Spartan princess with her muddy boots and halter top and long black braid. The stallion tosses his head as she leaps onto his back and yanks the reins.

The last time he visited her was at Easter, coming back from China. Now the leaves are turning as they ride along the bottom of a worn old mountain under this brilliant autumn sky. The iron shoes' hollow ring on Alabama rock remind him of the stone streets of his ruined cities. He follows right behind her, but the silence between them is as wide as a century. They stop to let their horses drink from a stream. "You can't come live with me in Europe," he says. "You hurt your mother when you talk like that."

She grins as though she just remembered a joke she wants to tell him. Then she shakes her head and looks his way. "You should know all about hurting her," she laughs, but there are tears in her eyes.

The creek bed is wide and shallow. Suddenly, she is circling him, prancing her horse like a Tennessee walker, splashing water everywhere.

"I'm never going to let anyone get to me," she tells him, driving her heels into Butterfly's flanks.

He takes off after her at a fool's dangerous gallop, arms flapping, bouncing so hard his teeth hurt. His gentle mare proves surprisingly fast along the winding trail, and he keeps his fleeing daughter in sight for the half mile through the woods.

She's a hundred feet ahead of him when they come into a field. A farmer's burning brushpile has sent a spark into dry grass. A wall of dancing flame blocks the way, spread by the wind, moving toward the pines—soon the whole forest will be ablaze.

He watches his fierce and heavenly daughter on her stallion charging back and forth in front of the inferno as she tries to decide the price of her pride and her pain. In those past worlds he inhabits, enemies are slain with golden daggers, slaves buried along with their masters, innocent hearts torn out in sacrifice to vain gods. And for once he thinks of the future, of all the men, young and old, who will go after her, crossing every bridge she will have set on fire behind her.

HAWAII

The pen in her hand is as useless as a dart thrown at wind, a flashlight shined at a phantom. She hasn't written a word since the day she learned where her father lived. She's read his telephone number for weeks like a code she has to crack.

She's always been at her best in winter when she can see what lies beneath the other seasons' extravagance. Her poems are crumbling sandstone, the twist of bare trees, frost that turns to steam on shingles in the morning sun.

"Mist it every day, preferably with rain water, but don't spray the buds," the woman at the plant store says. "It shouldn't get too hot: it shouldn't get too cold. Pamper it," the woman tells her, the one who once let a cactus die of neglect.

She takes the long way home, drives past the house in Crestline again. She remembers helping him across an entire summer. Each day he came home from the office and worked on the addition until dark. Using plans he'd ordered from the Whole Earth Catalogue, he built the greenhouse from scratch.

She parks, lets the motor idle to keep warm—there are flurries in the air and a promise of snow. No orchids grow behind steamy glass. Where an Eden once lured her into thinking that life would always stay the same, a family room now holds a wide screen television and children sent home early from school.

In Hoover, she opens the drapes in her mother's apartment. The crucifix is gone from the wall, carried to Mobile to hang in her grandmother's hospital room. She doesn't look where the photo albums are kept, the last twenty years trapped in scenes between clear vinyl pages. There's a shoe box hidden and a young couple dressed for a ball, the woman bending down to let the delighted little girl inhale her corsage.

Snow is falling as she carries the orchid inside her cabin and sets it in the sink. With a tuberous stem and dull leathery leaves, it isn't much to look at yet. Pale roots crawl from peat moss to the rim of the pot as though they want to drink her air. A reed-thin shoot with three fat buds has been tethered to a bamboo rod.

Her study is as spare as a monk's cell. Poised above a page so blank it hurts her eyes, she stares out the sliding glass door at the mountainside that has never failed to inspire her. She doesn't need to look at the pad beside the phone. She's memorized the number that will carry her question across a continent and half a shining sea and right through the gates of Paradise.

OAK

He tells me it's the biggest tree he's ever seen. It is, he says, a thing I'll never forget. This tree now stands in the yard of a house in a sprawling suburb far out on the edge of Birmingham. He tries to give me directions but the names of the streets don't come to him. Go here, turn right, another mile or so past the Interstate, then left. He tells me he doesn't get around like he used to, and it's been a few years since his last visit to the place. But he's certain the colossal oak endures. "It has been there forever," he says.

I have to use a pickax. The clay beneath the Southside lawn is packed with rubble. He stands with one hand holding onto the naked sapling while I carve out the hole. I can see him thinking of his tree, squinting at the chilly April sky.

As I work, I tell him about the tree of my childhood, a mammoth burr oak that stood by itself in the middle of a hundred- acre field. He nods, transplanted to another time, listening to the rush of those leaves.

I hack through roots, moist with a sweet river that flows toward the clouds. Then I hit fine sand. I fill his rusty wheelbarrow and empty it in the street where rain will wash the past back to the sea. I hear the old man sigh.

We finally plant the sapling, fill the hole with rich black loam from the hardware store and a bucket of bone meal. I let him do the final steps around the trunk and water with the hose. I notice him glancing at the sky again.

The old man wants to pay me but I refuse, so he fetches two lawn chairs and bottled Cokes and we settle in on either side of our oak, thinking of a breezy summer day a hundred years from now.

GRADUATION

No one sees her take the canoe. A few hard strokes and she knows she's not going to turn around, gliding away from the party lanterns into the moonless night. She paddles the way she learned at Bible camp a lifetime ago, switching sides every other stroke. She recalls what happened to Lot's wife, keeps the prow of her flimsy craft pointed dead ahead at the dark open lake and starry sky, but the music and the loud familiar voices follow her, unbreakable lines she cannot untie, chains attached to anchors.

She was so proud today, her eyes filled with tears, her last daughter behind the college podium giving the graduation speech. These past few years God has blessed her with answered prayers, her children all flying strong, money enough to buy this second home with a view. Already her arms are tired but she maintains a rhythm that she's found, no safety or security except what rides inside this shell. The noise from the party recedes, her daughter's favorite song played for the tenth time, blending with the splash her paddle makes and the knock of aluminum cutting through the water's breezy chop.

"You can have the world if you want it, Missy," Pappa used to tell her on those bright remembered mornings, the immense magnolia tree rising above the picnic table where he liked to take his coffee. It's her husband's dream to sell the house in town and retire here on the lake. The canoe was a housewarming present from his closest friend, a gift he's had no time to use. She stops to catch her breath, feels her heart pumping more than blood.

No lights shine on the opposite shore, the stars outlining those hills the power company owns. More than once she's looked through her husband's telescope, past the bass boats and water skiers. There's a rocky beach on a point graced by a grove of longleaf pines. One day a week ago she watched a young woman alone in a canoe stop to sunbathe there. At first, she felt ashamed, turned by her own dissatisfactions into a spy, feeding on someone else's life. She pried her eye away from the lens and returned to her housework. But two hours later the young woman was still there, sitting cross-legged on a blanket, staring out at a different panorama, dreaming a young woman's dreams.

The blade of the paddle stirs black water again. She goes until she feels and hears the bow slide up on stone. Wobbly, nearly falling in, she walks the length of the canoe and steps out on land. She can see little except the stars, the pines defined by their own darkness, the beach beneath her feet a lumpy treacherous sanctuary. Slowly and carefully, ignoring the nagging voice that warns her she will get mud on her new expensive dress, she turns around and sits, looking back across the lake where the view will never be the same.

CAVE

Carbide lamps give each face a halo. Caked with clay from the long crawl down the tunnel, they look like warriors in a Stone Age ceremony, their eyes as bright as candle flames behind the muddy masks.

A month on the indoor climbing wall has given him the confidence to go vertical. Chemo took its pounds of flesh but cured him. "Ranger Loco" they used to call him before he got sick—a Chicano kamikaze on a rope.

The others do the rigging, nylon lines so strong they could raise the dead. This cave on the Georgia line has just been discovered and they will be the first to go down. He walks to the edge of the pit, tosses a rock the size of a grapefruit and begins to count. The whole crew whistles when that boom of hollow thunder finally comes up over them.

He clips the carabiners to the bolts in the damp brown wall, adjusts the brake bars on the rack for the slowest ride. They hand him the seat sling, ready to go. Tied to four hundred feet of rope, he salutes them then lets himself down backwards into the dark. His wise Sonoran grandmother used to tell him stories about the spider who spins the thread by which we mortals dangle. The wall disappears once he's cleared the overhang and he floats in a space like the one before Genesis, where only God can keep him company. His name echoes. He shouts he's OK. Still so close to them he can see the aura of their lanterns up beyond the ledge, he knows he must let go, that falling is a mystery more to angels than to man.

He wonders what his 'caver' friends would say if they found out he used to be an altar boy. A good kid escaping the *barrio,* he couldn't wait to get inside the great cathedral, away from the loud and ugly world he knew too well. For a while he even thought he'd be a priest, but time and science took his faith away. He hasn't been to mass in twenty years. He was always sure he'd face death bravely, the same way he used to fly down a rope. He remembers the last trip to Mexico—that thousand-foot plunge into the black belly of *Santo de las Golandrinas,* the world's deepest pit. Some doctors say they never get used to patients dying, but he did, a risk every oncologist runs. Then he found the lump under his own arm. "Are you going to hang around forever?" someone yells, the question coming back a dozen times.

A child of a mammoth city in lust with light, he never got accustomed to real darkness. One time the social workers took them to a country camp and he had to sleep in a terrifying room where he couldn't see his hand in front of his face. He crawled past the bunks to the heavy door and jimmied the latch open. Outside the moonless night blinked with a million yellow sparks. As he ran jumping and twirling through fireflies, he promised he would never doubt what his grandmother said about the Holy Spirit.

He relaxes the grip his braking hand has on the rope and lets it slide through his fingers. What glow is left above him is quickly swallowed, his line vanishing into the starless sky. He tries to remember all the words as he descends, Latin the perfect subterranean tongue. When he touches down on dusty ground, he lets off one of the old Ranger Loco war whoops. Distant cheers rain from another time. He watches the sling rise up and disappear, gone for its next soul. On shaky legs he begins to explore, walking into a side chamber that turns into a sparkling grotto filled with gypsum needles and pedestals of flow stone. "*Sanctus*," he says, his voice becoming song.

"*Sanctus, Sanctus, Sanctus.*" And the rest of the words come back to him as though he'd knelt at an altar yesterday.

BLACKBERRY SUMMER

He sees her across the room. Even though he has never left town, this is his first reunion. The other familiar high school faces blur into the crowd as his heart focuses his eyes.

Over the years he has gathered news from her odyssey, a mental scrapbook of facts and hearsay and malicious gossip filtered through a sympathy that only grows with his own failures and pain. Her last divorce coincided with his own.

He has not seen her since graduation night. The next morning, she was gone for good, her wild seeds demanding to be sown far and wide. Many times, he has imagined the children they might have had—blond and curly headed like her. Now she wears her hair cut short and combed like a man's, tinged with fashionable red in the ballroom light. She smokes a thin cigarette.

Once again, he thinks of that day when they were six years old. While their mothers baked pies, he wandered with her into the afternoon. All along the edge of the woods, brambles lowered their arms to welcome them. Berries dark as raven's eyes glistened in the sun.

He had been the one to reach for the fruit. He jerked back his hand with a cry—a thorn had pierced his finger. Never before had he known that his body coursed with blood, or that shedding tears in front of another could make his face burn with shame. Calmly, delicately, she picked a blackberry and put it in her mouth. Even then, he loved her. Still chewing, she turned to him and came so close his eyes crossed as he looked into hers. Her lips warm, and sweet mixed with bitter, she kissed him.

He does not cross the gulf between them yet, but takes a long drink from his whisky. He considers walking out now, letting the past rest and the future continue on its present course, unaffected by this near encounter with the woman who taught him a life's worth of lessons on suffering before he'd even become a man.

But he begins to move forward, toward her, because with one prick of a thorn that afternoon, and the taste of blackberry in her mouth, he'd come to know even more about temptation.

HONEY

I linger among the bees flying in and out of the numerous hives lining the side yard by the alley. It's a sunny late afternoon and each bee wears a halo. I imagine them foraging the overgrown yards of abandoned houses, and the weeds the railroad doesn't bother to fight anymore, and the thickets along the potholed streets the city no longer maintains. I assume the owners of the property have lived here since that time when the neighborhood was vibrant with families who worked in the vanished factories. They have a sign on a tree in front saying "Honey For Sale."

A couple is sitting on the porch and I introduce myself. They are barely middle-aged, the man with a beard and shaggy hair, the woman in a long gingham dress spread between her knees to catch the beans she snaps, the way my grandmother did. "How did you get interested in beekeeping?" I ask.

"My parents were country folks who moved here so my father could work in the mills," the man says. "My mother's people kept bees, so there were always a few hives in the yard and enough honey to last the winter. When my parents passed, we decided to move back from San Francisco and put roots down here. One thing led to another," he laughs.

I tell them about the tree in the woods of my boyhood, a hollow sycamore inhabited by wild bees that crowded constantly through a small hole. Every time I went on my rambles I would stop at the tree and put my ear against its side and listen.

"The ancients knew the bee to represent goddesses and gods," the woman explains. "The hum of its wings is a prophecy, its voice the very sound of creation." She pours a rain of beans from her lap into a pan and tells me she teaches English at the local college. "The Scottish say to ask the wild bee for what the druids knew."

The three of us walk around the house to a long shed with weathered siding. Inside wait the implements of the beekeeper's trade—the helmets with their drooping veils, thick pairs of gloves stained by pollen, wax, and royal jelly; there are bee brushes and fume boards, strainers and feeders, uncapping tools and a smoker hanging from a nail. In the middle of the floor stands the extractor, its handle begging to be cranked. The man has placed old photos of the neighborhood in its prime all around, and on the far side of the room, in good light, the Monet-like paintings of flowers and gardens he has done.

When the woman brings me a golden jar of spring honey, I know what the bees were telling me in that hollow tree so long ago, what these people here in front of me are certain of—there is still magic in the world, and there is still hope.

COAL

She does not look at the snake skins hanging in a line from his book shelf. The animal pelts disturb her a little less—Mountain Brook road kills, skinned and nailed to plywood in the garage and tanned with Morton's salt. A possum hide, pale as death, covers the keyboard of the computer he no longer uses.

She has promised to look after the aquarium while he is away with his father at a Scout jamboree in North Alabama. The water has turned green over the past weeks—the exact color of his eyes. She bends down carefully with one hand beneath her stomach. Her daughter is due in a month.

Shapes move, their tails nearly shrunken away. Those arms and legs that sprouted like beans when the water was clear now stroke perfectly formed with spidery fingers and toes. She remembers the sunny afternoon and her son with his scoop and bucket, walking in boots through shallow water. Up on a rise, safe from the swamp, she felt the shrill piping of a million frogs penetrate her skin, a music you would hear only under the spell of fever.

She sprinkles fish food for the tadpoles and picks up the dirty clothes scattered across the floor. In one corner she notices a cardboard box filled to the top with darkness. She lowers herself again. The baby shifts against her heart.

The chunk of coal is shiny and cold in her hand, and she wonders why he has gathered so much of it and where he found it. She knows from high school science that coal is something ancient once alive: she remembers ferns the size of trees, dragonflies as long as her arms.

A friend, a New Age mystic type, says her son is an old soul—dozens, hundreds, even thousands of lives rolling down through time like a snowball of reincarnation. Sometimes when she watches him as he sits in his silent concentration, his eyes like far away reflections of green summer forest, she sees glimpses of what might be those others. or simply himself, a self much too complicated to stay inside the body of a boy. Like all mothers, she worries for the future.

She would love to make her son's life roll down a smooth road in the best of weather. But this coal in her hand, heavy and cold and filled with mystery, terrifies her.

She stands and the contractions start again. She must sit down to rest on her son's unmade bed. In their green water the big tadpoles swirl, almost grown. Soon he will carry them down to the creek by the golf course and set them free. Her son, such a strange young man—she knows he has much to teach her.

ICARUS

He stops at the airplane crash. Thousands of hands over thirty years have taken their souvenirs—all that remain are aluminum bones too big to carry off the mountain, unwieldy pieces of body and wing someone has arranged into a metal cairn.

He hasn't bought a Porsche. He hasn't left his wife for a younger woman, or cashed his chips for a sailboat in the Keys. Yesterday he smiled at the jokes, the witty cards that came, the roasting he got at his own party. "Fifty isn't old these days," they reassured him after they had their fun. At the window in the Summit Club he held a champagne glass to the setting sun and saw how endless strings of pearls unwind from nothing.

The Blue Trail twines through a whorl of elevation lines on the topo map. He tries to remember the last time he came up here, long ago with his children. He re-ties the hiking boots that are a birthday gift from his eldest son and thinks of when his own father took him along to New York City. "Now you can say you've already been to the top," his father joked as they stood at the tip of the Empire State Building, their eyes caught in the labyrinth of Manhattan. That was the moment he knew what he wanted to do with his life—direction, road, and destination in one huge flash.

On the way to Oak Mountain he'd driven past the site of the new complex he's designed, a hundred acres cleaned to a palette of red clay. Swerving off 280 he sat in the middle of his latest dream, the white buildings rising from his imagination to reflect the April light. He continues along the trail, dogwoods blooming around him, the forest turning greener by the minute as though time followed the call of life instead of the opposite. He's wearing the same rucksack he carried across Europe as student, olive canvas grimed with the smoke and dust of Rome and Athens. Hawk Cliff is marked on the map, the lines of the fingerprint narrowly parallel where the ridge drops away. Climbing up on lichen-covered rocks he looks out on a valley where streets will someday cast a net and office towers gleam above the unbroken trees.

He sits and removes his sketch pad and pen. A buzzard circles high into the sun. An architect, he's always been too busy in the maze he makes, too trapped by puzzles and walls to concern himself with flying. Daedalus and Icarus, he recalls, escaped the Labyrinth with wings. He draws one mark across the page, like the horizon he sees in front of him, and thinks of Minotaurs and boys falling into the sea. The sky, he suspects with a smile, belongs to old men.

THE FOURTH OF JULY

He thinks he'll drive all night and make it to Alabama but gets a room just outside of Chattanooga. He bought the notebook over a month ago, the large university kind with hard green cover and no lines on the pages. He's written nothing, not even a letter, since he dropped out of the MFA program at Iowa in 1994.

He dreams again about Desert Storm, about those stretches of sand as flat as a sea. He's always alone, far from the safety of tanks and choppers and proud flags flying in that dry cold wind. In the dreams something always calls him away from his comrades, pulls him like a sleepwalker out into that no man's land where he finds himself wandering—lost without a weapon, no water or food and no idea which direction to go.

Waking early before the heat he showers, drives to the top of Lookout Mountain, gazing south into the summer haze. "Your granddaddy's not feeling well so we're glad you're coming home," his mother told him yesterday on the phone, the real message hidden in code beneath her eternal good cheer.

He envied the guys from 'Nam, much more a writer's war than the fast forward blitzkrieg that blew away Saddam's dark legions. "Maybe you are trying too hard," his favorite teacher at Iowa advised him more than once. "And maybe you're exploring the wrong territory." He winds on back roads with his windows down, listening to a country station from Fort Payne, comes to the blue reach of Lake Guntersville and goes for a swim. Drying himself with a motel towel, he thinks how he never let the old man baptize him. During all those Sunday mornings, through all those revival meetings and camps, he never allowed himself to take the plunge, to be immersed, as they said, "in that watery grave." There's a Fourth of July parade through Boaz and as he watches the marching bands mixed with veterans and small-town celebrities he wonders if he'll ever feel at home anywhere.

The roadside park is just the same, the cars newer, his kin more numerous than ever. A knot of children set off firecrackers in the parking lot. His grandfather's little church shines immaculately white across the pasture. Through barbecue smoke he sees the old man sitting in a wheelchair, his mother on the other side of the crowd talking to her sister. Thirsty, and not quite able to cross these last few intimate yards of gravel and grass, he heads up the path toward the spring.

As the story goes, before taking up the Lord's work, his grandfather had been the best well dowser in Blount County. One year during a terrible drought the someday preacher cut a fork from a willow tree in the family graveyard, held it in his hands and asked to be led to a source that would never run dry. When they sank the pipe at the spot where the divining rod broke in two, they hit an artesian vein. The little stream beside the trail still runs cold and clear, lined by ferns and darting with dragonflies.

He kneels and cups his hands under the mossy pipe, drinks the water that faintly tastes of brimstone and iron until he can't hold any more. The day he left Kuwait he took a jeep and drove one last time through a wasteland empty except for sand and pillars of fire. He walks back to edge of the woods but doesn't enter the open yet. Instead he sits and writes the first long sentence in his notebook, the one about a soldier from Alabama and Moses striking the rock and another kind of war fought within the province of the heart.

BLACKBIRDS

A familiar noise lifts him from his nap. On this still and sunny winter afternoon a great wind has suddenly arrived. He rolls from the bunk bed just as all the windows around the one-room cabin darken—a blizzard of black wings, a spinning screeching cyclone.

He has come here to the middle of nowhere to escape himself. Seven months of true love have earned him lessons he thought he had already mastered. He tiptoes across the plank floor and peers through glass. Ten thousand grackles settle in for lunch.

If she were here, they would marvel how nature so confidently replicates itself. "Life delights in life," said Blake, her favorite. Ten thousand birds rummage through dead leaves and it sounds like fire burning. Would the ache in his heart go away if he knew such companionship?

He remembers the BB gun he got for Christmas and the first thing he killed. Limp and warm in his hand, it had fallen too hard from the tip of the tree to be a creature that flew so easily. The son of a hunter he had felt no sadness or remorse, only fascination at the iridescent shimmer of the male grackle's black feathers up close, the rainbow gasoline makes spreading across a puddle.

He thinks of sitting between his parents on the way to church. How he would brace himself every Sunday as they neared the undulating spot his father called "the big dipper." Accelerating up the slope he can hear his siblings in the back seat screaming with delight while he grimly clutches his mother's arm. At the top, as the road falls away, they lose all their weight, slamming down one eternal moment later on the pavement again, somehow heavier than before.

There are paintings by Chagall where everything alive leaves the earth and rises—chickens, sheep, rabbis and lovers sailing high above the Russian plain. It still frightens him at night when, half asleep, he feels that drop, as if he had floated an inch or two above the bed as his conscious mind receded.

He listens to grackles on the roof, pecking at the little acorns of the water oak that keeps its green leaves even in January. He looks over his shoulder at the table and the letter he is writing, the page complete except for the last line and his signature. As he walks across the rough wood floor in his runner's socks, he feels the constant tug of gravity, this life on earth and the load we must all bear. He crumples the letter and tosses it into the ashes of last night's fire.

At the door he takes the last breath as a coward. Hand on the latch, he lets his heart go racing. Stepping out into the light and the slap of the cold the whole world breaks loose. Ten thousand grackles take off at once, a dark storm of miraculous panic with no use for rumination. He rises with them.

THE SURFACE OF THE MOON

It's the brightest moon she's ever seen. A warm front just moved in from the Gulf has turned a cold December day into a balmy night. The same south wind that lifted morning palms like skirts now mixes moonlight and pine trees into a shadow dance on her bedroom wall. She tries to sleep but feels her spirit whirling like a dervish.

She calculates the hour in Munich, calls her fiancé who's getting dressed for his final meeting. She describes the night, the moon, her crazy mood, and he tells her she's the most beautiful girl in the world.

"I wish you could see yourself as I do," he says. Even across the gulf of space she can hear that little tremble in his voice. "Promise me something," he asks, and she does.

She rolls out of bed, casts her own shade in the lunar glow, pausing to study her body's silhouette, suddenly ashamed how vain a woman has to be in this world of surfaces. She kneels and twists herself around her arms and hands, changing into different beasts on the luminous wall, the same game she played with herself as a girl, the feminine forever shifting shapes.

Up east at school she'd used the web of southern charm, a trap door spider if she had to be. There were those who couldn't believe she'd come on an athletic scholarship; she had no doubters when they saw her on the tennis court. And all the rich New England boys who thought they got the belle of the ball needed to be taken down a notch or two.

Downstairs the amber darkroom bulb reminds her of the shine that penetrates an eyelid closed against the summer sun—strong light through skin and rushing blood. She chooses a camera and loads a roll of special film.

The latest shots from the nursing home still hang to dry on the wire above the developing pans. She studies them, done in black and white, each woman's face so close it fills the frame. Food and fashion, portraits and weddings pay her bills, but these old ladies she photographs for some reason she cannot name, perhaps the same one she knows would make her look inside Pandora's Box or want to learn the day she is to die.

Barefoot, in a sheer satin gown, she walks outside toward the swing where he proposed. The moonlight hasn't warmed the grass. She hesitates to shoot herself—she's never done a self-portrait. Traveling abroad one summer with a friend, her first good camera in her hand and her eyes in love with everything she saw, she made the jitney driver stop in a Turkish village. Turkish women wore no veils, but the beautiful one at the well turned and ran inside when the Nikon came out.

"They believe you steal their souls," the driver said. She unfolds the tripod in front of the swing. The light falls so hard from the sky she can read the f-stops. Reaching in the camera bag, she twists on a telephoto lens, aiming up at the ancient goddess of the night. Before she poses for the shot she promised her lover, she thinks of the women at the nursing home as she zeroes in and photographs the surface of moon.

HORNET'S NEST

All summer long they've kept each other company, the artist and his nest of hornets. Good day and bad, he's sketched the progress of their world, from hanging clump of parchment cells to paper moon the size of a basketball.

He views his life as a trip through the labyrinth. Each and every thing in his world, he says, can serve as a key. He's a man of odd and singular preoccupations. One year he spent collecting fossils from a river bed, another year bones were his obsession. I came to visit once and found the terrible skeleton of a cat standing upright on his kitchen table, dressed for Mardi Gras. By now his friends should know what they are getting.

He shows me hornets drawn from every angle, meticulous renderings more like schematic plans than art. He says he needs to work this way at first to understand his own strange captivation. Later on, freed from the chains of detail and document, he will soar.

At summer's end the nest is huge behind his garage. Hornet traffic fills the air, streaming back and forth without concern. We peer through a window to avoid getting stung. "I'm still not sure what I'm supposed to learn," he says.

Autumn is rainy at first. My friend stays in his studio, poring over slides and reading books on entomology. He tells me how the queen's last eggs miraculously turn into other queens and drones, who fly off and mate in the sky, never to return. With nothing left to do, the worker hornets drift away, while the old queen, body spent and hungry, roams her empty chambers.

Mid-October brings the sun again and dry cool days down from the north. I call my friend one morning, but his wife says he has disappeared. "Nothing to be concerned about at this point," she assures, an expert in his ways.

A week goes by, then two. I wander over and check his padlocked studio. In a spiderweb by the door, three dead hornets float, neatly wrapped in silk. Out back I check the nest, still hanging from its branch, but lifeless now, a paper lantern left to tatter in the wind.

My phone rings the day before Halloween. The artist has returned. Would I please come by and see something, he asks? He ushers me in without a word, whips a sheet from a canvas the size of a door. In hues too rich to describe, with details fastidious yet liberating as my eyes begin to understand their pattern, he has painted a map that leads him back to his sanity.

LIGHTNING

He thinks of many things that must steep in time before they can be used. Inside the shed he can no longer smell the storm, wet and broken and tingling sweet with ozone. Five years is what the lumber yard told him. Oak needs five years.

He takes down a board as long as a man. Still rough, it reminds him of old barns the settlers built, homeplaces cut from the forest, dreams sunk like wells into the soil.

They bought this place when he was still a resident. She loved the wild meadow and the trees. This is where they were going to put down roots, raise their family. They promised themselves they would never leave.

He always laughed at jokes about psychiatrists, the blind leading the blind, they said. More than once an older patient looked at him aghast—could someone so young possibly know? He studies pictures of himself back then; zeal paired with innocence conquers all and science is like an eye without a body.

Cancer took the long way, leading them over mountains of hope. They tried everything to save her but in the end she simply fell asleep.

When he left the hospital, it was as if he had turned to shadow, every bit of his substance drained. Closing his eyes in the parking lot he could feel the sun shine straight through him. The director of the funeral home held his hand and whispered "the next world is a realm of unimaginable light."

He shunned the pills that would have helped his appetite and sleep. Alone in the house he quit eating altogether, drank water only if his lips began to bleed. The day he fainted on the ward they made him check in for tests and kept him for a week.

His first night home thunder woke him, snapped the fragile thread they'd used to sew him back together. Stumbling out into the teeth of the storm he felt the very bottom soft and cold beneath his feet, and when he slipped in the mud and fell he knew he would never get up again.

The first bolt came down and hit the power line, popping green fire like a Roman candle. The second curled like a scorpion's tail, stabbing the black woods behind the house. The third bolt came down straight and broke into a brilliant cage that fell around the old white oak under which he lay.

After much consideration, he thinks the current passed through him. He remembers nothing but a flash and waking up in the rain, a hundred feet of tree stretched out next to him.

The day after the storm, he called a man with a portable saw mill and had the oak cut into lumber that he stored away, wet with sap and rain and smelling like barrels ready for new wine.

He carries the long board into his shop. He runs it through the planer, then sands one side smooth as skin. Like a blind man reading braille, his fingers move along the grain. Pouring linseed oil on a rag, he rubs it in, bringing out the rippling lines and whorls that remind him of those photographs of the surface of the sun. Oak, cured for five year—now he can start on baby cradles, rocking chairs, and a grandfather clock...or that long kitchen table his new love wants, wedding presents for another life.

ORIGAMI

They begin filling up balloons. He slides the latex ring over the stem of the tank, turns the valve, hands the finished product to his daughter who ties the string. The next one he holds to his mouth, inhales the dry cool gas that lets him say her name in a cartoon voice.

She looks so much like her mother, those pale blue eyes nothing can perturb, those long fingers already playing the violin. "You're silly, daddy," she tells him, but he already knows how love can turn a man into a clown.

He sees now the mistakes he made, hindsight with its terrible clarity panning through the wreckage. The year he's lived alone has taught him the language of silence and how powerful the currents are that run just beneath life's ordinary surface.

She ties another balloon, lets it bump against the ceiling. He bought two packages of balloons and they have the whole day before he has to take her back. "Is your mamma still dating Jim?" he asks her and she nods her head.

They stop for lunch. Outside the trailer he's got a little garden, three Big Boy tomatoes covering a chicken wire trellis, one hot pepper and a basil plant as tall as a bush. He passes on the chili, whips up a sauce for two plates of spaghetti.

"Exactly why do balloons float?" she asks him, wiping the corner of her mouth with the tip of her napkin just the way her mother does. It's the kind of question every father dreads, so direct and basic that only a scientist can answer it. "Something to do with helium being lighter than air, honey," he says. "I'll look it up and tell you next week."

He washes the dishes, she dries. "Why don't you date anyone?" she asks. Underneath the suds his hands search for forks and spoons. "Because I still love your mother, I guess," he says. They fill the rest of the balloons, so many of them they cover the ceiling, jostling and bumping like a waiting crowd every time the AC kicks in. "What are we going to do with all these balloons?" he asks. "I know," she says, her beautiful eyes blinking slow as a Persian cat's.

He keeps construction paper and crayons, scissors and glue, although lately she seems to have outgrown that stage. She spreads everything out on the table in the eating nook, her long fingers careful and meticulous with their pink nail polish. "Where did you learn how to do that?" he asks.

"Jim showed me. It's called origami," she says as she puts the finishing touches on her delicate creation, part bird, part boat, decorated in all the colors of the rainbow. The lump in his throat feels as big as an apple. He wants to take her home right now, give her back to Jim, take a lighted cigarette and pop all these stupid balloons.

He goes to the bathroom, washes his face, nearly breaks the mirror with his fist. Back at the table she's cut three figures out of paper, given them eyes, noses and smiles. "Mommy, you, and me," she grins, holding each one up for him to see. Her bird boat has a loop like a basket. She ties on balloon after balloon until it won't stay down.

Outside the afternoon thunderheads are billowing in the west, high and blinding white like the mountains of Heaven. She counts down from ten then lets it go, and he knows the wish he makes is impossible as he watches the three of them in their ark dwindle to a dot, then disappear.

CROW

He opens the deerskin pouch and explains the power of the objects held inside. He shows us minerals, a piece of bone, a tuft of buffalo hair. The Australian couple videotapes his every move. He is giving them this gift to take back home to their grandson.

He speaks in a voice so gentle we strain to hear him above the wind outside his trailer. "When you feel all by yourself in the world, take out these things and arrange them in a circle," he tells the camera and an enchanted boy twelve thousand miles away.

I imagined he would be much older, grey hair in braids, a sun-wizened shaman like the ones in Carlos Casteñada books. But this *Yaqui* medicine man looks barely forty and lives in a mobile home in the rocky hills not far from Birmingham. He tells us about the grandfather who raised him in the Arizona desert, about all the generations of his family who have answered the call. My wonder and my doubt chase each other around a room where the wrong time flashes on a VCR and the walls are hung with coyote pelts and magic feathers.

As a child, he says he climbed the trees where crows built their nests. Crows have very strong spirits and know how to steal treasures the world hides from those possessed by greed and folly.

Inside his trailer all the tables are covered with Nature's loot. He hands us crystals that knit bone, a leaf that becomes an eagle, acorns that can raise the dead. We feel our fingers tingling. The blood in our ears sings like the red-winged blackbird.

The Australians ask him about emptiness and loss, why the center of our modern life does not hold. He takes off a silver ring his grandfather gave him and puts it in the man's hand. "The ring is no longer on my finger," he says. "But if you carry it to the bottom of the earth, I would still be connected to what's mine." He describes the invisible threads that bind everything together, Spider Woman busy at her web.

The wind dies and we walk outside. He tells us how he came to Alabama to visit a brother, and how he stayed because he liked tall trees. Below the trailer, among poplar and pine, he shows us his sweat lodge, a dome built of branches, the pit where hot stones give up their visions. He talks of his work among his people—Cherokee, Osage, Sioux. Further down the hill, he points to the creek where the Old Ones bathe when they visit, driving back across America in their ancient pickups, those Fords and Chevys eaten away by salt.

Just before we leave, he invites us to watch him make a dream catcher. Inside a leather-covered ring, he weaves a cat's cradle string, looping it with nimble fingers to hold bits of glass and colored beads, pebbles and shells. Gathered around, we watch the hole in the middle grow smaller and smaller, until he laughs a crow's laugh and pulls the circle closed.

PRODIGAL SON

Downstairs at three in the morning the Christmas tree still sparkles and blinks. The long flight from California, all the pecan pie and eggnog—he can't fall asleep.

He hasn't been home since his father's funeral. The big leather easy chair still faces the hearth, molded to the old man's shape. He cleans off children's toys and wrapping paper and slides down into those retirement years, fragrant with smoke and Old Spice aftershave. He dozes off, dreams of the old house in Fairfield and the happy part of growing up.

He wakes to the sound of neighborhood dogs and light the color of a cold sea. The fireplace stands as tall as a man, made to his father's specifications when they built this house in Mountain Brook. The pain nearly overwhelms him. It pours down the chimney from the empty Christmas sky. Outside the dampness sinks into his desert-tempered bones. He briefly thinks of driving to the airport and catching the next plane back to L.A. In the movies there is always one last chance to make things right, to close the wounds and say what should be said. He wonders if his father forgave him.

The long garage stands at the back of the property. Built of stone, like the house, it waits the return of a man who made his own furniture, who shoveled Pennsylvania coal as a boy and worked his way to Birmingham to give his life to steel.

Everything is gone, benches, tools, the lumber stacked among the rafters as if a flood might come. He curses his brothers for not telling him; but why should he care, the prodigal son, always floating high above the family squabbles, thumbing his nose.

He opens the door to the room in back and discovers it filled with ax-split cords of hickory and oak. There's even kindling, pared with a hatchet down to the width of a match, all the different sizes neatly bundled and tied in twine by a man who knew how to make a fire. He gathers what he needs and returns to the house.

The andirons have been scrubbed clean of soot. Someone has patched the scorched and crumbling mortar between the bricks. He begins to arrange the tinder, lattice upon lattice, each layer bringing him another memory. Once, when he was ten, just the two of them went camping on a now forgotten river. He remembers the campfire burning down to a pile of rubies in the night and how he wanted to stay by his father's side forever.

The flame climbs into the wood, singing with the voice of release. He carries in log after log and eats his mother's biscuits in front of a roaring fire.

Waiting for the rest of the family to arrive, he sits in his father's chair, worn out from his travel, but slowly filling with a warmth he hopes will never leave.

MARCH

The moving van takes away the last of her belongings. He stands at the window, watching it vanish up the hill. In these bare white rooms, thoughts echo and he can't find any words.

Divorce has left a roof over his head. Yesterday it rained and he lay for hours on his futon, listening to a sound that can wear down mountains. Today the sun shines on this final exodus. He knows he is about to go into the desert alone.

One spring morning, during the best of times, he had carried two rings in his pocket—plain golden bands, simple and pure, like love meant to be. He married her in the Japanese Garden, beneath a cherry tree in full blossom. That night in Aspen, while his new wife slept, the lone white petal she had carried in her hair, all the way from Alabama, made his eyes well with strange tears.

All his life he has struggled to remain in that level place between joy and pain. Now he cringes with every clap of thunder or woman's smile, and a nameless, breathless feeling rides with him in elevators. He hears his ex-wife's absence in every creak of the floor. The counselor he sees talks of grieving as if it were as simple as a jump into the deep end of the pool.

The ring still glows on his finger. He thinks of his parent's long marriage, of his grandmother and grandfather buried side by side, how gold dug from tombs three thousand years old shines uncorrupted by the sadness of time.

His grandmother was a country woman. Every March, his grandfather would prepare her garden, turning up the ground with a short-handled spade. He remembers the smell of fresh, damp dirt and the redworms and night crawlers he gathered in a coffee can to carry down to the Shades Creek. His grandmother always let him sit at her kitchen table while she chose what seeds to sow, each packet a cornucopia that would soon spill from a source he could not quite comprehend.

He turns away from the window and walks through the house to the garage. The shovel still has a price tag stuck to its polished blade, bought for chores he never got around to doing. It feels too light in his hands, so unlike the heavy iron tools his grandfather used. Outside, under the sky, he has a momentary surge of the elevator panic—all his weight gone and no anchor. But he goes to the middle of the lawn, still unsure why he needs to dig a hole.

He presses one foot on the shovel and cuts down through matted grass beginning to green. The earth does not turn easily the first time. He drives the shovel in with both feet, grunts, and wrenches the handle with all his strength. The rocky soil gives. He digs as hard and fast as he can until the thoughts no longer run wild in his head and he slumps against the handle, staring at what he has done.

On his knees, he inhales the smell of childhood and new graves. He leans forward and reaches into the hole with his left hand, down into coolness and shadow, letting it loosen the lock that encircles his heart. He slips off the wedding ring with his thumb and pushes and scrapes the pile of loose dirt and stones back in, until the wound he opened is sealed. Shaking and exhausted, he turns over on his back, lying there on the grass, on this sad little ball spinning through darkness, and then he knows he will very soon learn how to weep.

RIVER TREASURE

A friend tells me about a recent dream. He dives into the deep bend of a river and discovers the sandy bottom littered with jewels. "I was afraid to touch them," he confesses as we jog around the track at UAB.

I am going fishing on the Cahaba and invite him along. We find a promising spot not far from where the city of Birmingham draws water. We begin casting golden lures the size and shape of scarab beetles into the current—as we reel them near to the shore we can see them scintillating just beneath the surface.

I tell my friend how my father used to take me to a river near our home. Always, we still-fished with dough balls, hardly speaking, our rods cradled in forked sticks driven into the muddy bank, our motionless lines disappearing into the dark slow water. We never seemed to catch fish, a fact that drove me to desperation, and one that didn't appear to bother my father in the slightest.

My friend asks me if it's difficult living alone. He is going through a divorce and has no children. I try hard to give him an honest answer, but the truth is elusive, sometimes daring me with its brightness, sometimes creeping in, perfectly disguised, to feed on my heart.

My friend and I catch no fish. We sit on the piling of a vanished bridge and talk. A kingfisher cackles and dives, flying up to taunt us with a silver prize for its bravery. Nine green canoes glide past on the sunny current. "Where are you going?" my friend calls out. "To see the Cahaba lilies," the lead man answers; he is wearing a wide straw hat and short red beard and looks like Van Gogh. This all seems to make my friend even sadder.

A stream feeds into the river nearby. Its narrow delta is cluttered with stones. I take off my shoes and wade through the shallow water, the way I did as a boy while my father fished. I gather rocks in my hat until it is filled, then put them all back except for one.On the river's edge my friend is staring into a blank murky flood pooling at his feet. "I found something for you," I tell him, but we need the hammer in the trunk of my car.

It is an old hammer from my father's toolbox. I put the lumpish brown wart-covered stone on the pavement and tap it until it breaks in two. Then I hand it over to my friend, who stares at the glittering amethyst wonder of its hollow core as though he's never seen a geode.

MINE

She fills the gourd with her mother's pearls, a piece of coal smashed to bits, seeds of her favorite flower—the morning glory. She adds the diamond from her first wedding ring and the letter beads from the bracelet they put around her wrist the day she was born—the name given to her by this world, not the name she will learn when she takes her last breath.

She seals the gourd but does not shake it. The gourd woman who taught a guest class at the art center said to paint it with your soul. She thinks of Hopi kachina rattles, loud little thunder makers covered with lightning and filled with corn. "The rattle is the oldest instrument and the most powerful," the gourd woman at the gallery explained. "The first human discovered the rattle when she picked up a coyote skull filled with little stones the ants carried in." She mixes paint until the color matches the sky right before dawn. "Just like wings opening," her father used to say, standing on the front porch facing east, ready to go down into the Mulga mines.

She covers the rattle with a coating of night about to end, a night outside the city and thick with stars. She recites the planets' names and all the constellations. There are many other names her father taught her—always naming, always that sad longing to know. With a fine-tipped brush she adds the Alabama moon in all its phases, the moon that made him love her mother, the moon that floods her with its tide.

Her Southside bungalow, filled with books, is no consolation now. Her bones have been gnawed by loneliness into desert shapes, whistling buttes and haunted mesas where her memories prowl. Soon she will wear down flat and sand will hiss as it drifts in the wind.

She cancels her appointments; tells her lover she is ill. With the rattle on the seat beside her, she drives across town to the nursing home, its name like a children's story of a happy life ahead with a pleasant ending.

He doesn't wake these days. She scoots the tank up next to his bed and runs her hand along the tube feeding him oxygen, listening to the air as it enters and leaves his damaged lungs. She slips the rattle from her purse and puts its handle in his bony hand. How she wishes he would open his eyes, the strong man who came home every evening black with dust, and shake it for her. But she must be the one.

PEACHES

Early sunlight gently wakes him on the couch, a golden moment filtered through the lashes of his eyes. Then he remembers last night. He tries to sit up but a poison has worked on every cell—it's the worst fight they've ever had. "Everything I do is wrong!" she cried, slamming the bedroom door, the snapping lock driving home an awful point. He lies with his hands pressed over his face, watching the same scenes replay on a dark screen of regret.

The voices of doom tell him this can never work, that passion so profound always ends in ashes. "What can be the harm in waiting?" his father counseled, never one to press advice. They got married on the fly. Like lovers in a reckless movie they drove down to a little Black Belt town, took their vows before a white-haired judge and spent their weekend honeymoon on Bourbon Street.

He knows he has to stand but once on his feet there's nowhere to go. He ponders knocking on the bedroom door but then those things she said last night begin to rise from the dead. He wonders if she could be right, if the way he's always seen himself is nothing more than unenlightened self-deceit. Gazing in the bathroom mirror he hopes for a glimpse of the arrogant prig, of the rigid snob who's always right, of the petty household tyrant who she says hides behind that boyish face. A stab of hunger reminds him they never got around to dinner. Two choice chops of lamb still wait in their marinade pan inside the Frigidaire, two sad bowls of salad have wilted on the counter by the sink.

It all started with the peaches she brought home, peaches he was going to use to make a pie. Even from a distance he could tell they were green, the meat beneath their unripe skin as hard and sour as a quince. The empty box lies on its side on the floor where she threw it, peaches scattered everywhere like the curious playing balls of some unwinnable game, a game requiring too much luck and not enough skill. He kneels and begins to gather them from the tile, the tile he chose and laid himself and waxes every Saturday whether it needs it or not. One of the peaches yields to his touch, perfectly ripe but badly bruised. A few more hours and it won't be fit to eat. Suddenly he knows he must change.

Outside the birds are loud with morning, with the simple joy that fuels the machinery of Creation. Resting the stepladder against the house, he undoes the screws holding the screen. She sleeps half sitting up on pillows behind her back. He hesitates, spellbound by what he's discovered. Every breath she takes is magnified by her pregnant stomach, the hefty T-shirt of his she wears to bed stretched tight by the miracle they have somehow managed to work together.

He climbs in, sits down so carefully on the bed, runs his finger lightly down her cheek, kisses her even lighter on the forehead, on each eyelid more lightly still. As she wakes, he has the first piece ready. "Now hush," he says as she starts to protest, gently feeding her a slice of peach.

JUMPER

He watches the airplane pass overhead, climbing until it's only a speck in the eastern sky. He fears he's misunderstood her directions, but then he sees the plane bank left, suddenly a star as it reflects the sun. It circles back toward him.

The memory of her in a wheelchair is still as fresh as newly shattered bone. "She may never fully recover," the doctor warned.

He'd met the insurance adjustor at the salvage yard to see for himself what remained of her new car. A jagged hole gaped in the roof where they cut her from the wreckage. Running his finger hard along one of those sharp edges, he had drawn his own blood.

The sound of the plane's engine is high and confident as it approaches. Today is the first cool day in months, and he is amazed how clear the air is above the Shelby County hills.

"I'll be the one wearing a red jumpsuit," she'd said. He thinks of that day on their honeymoon, hiking up the Jungfrau in the Swiss Alps. She leaped the guardrail, ignoring warning signs in four languages, to stand on the edge of a precipice overlooking the most beautiful valley either of them had ever seen. She motioned for him to follow, but heights terrified him—but not as much as the thought of losing her. The photo she took now hangs above their bed.

"It can't be as dangerous as driving a car," she laughed when she told him the way she intended to celebrate the anniversary of the crash. He tries to find the plane in the binoculars, but the blue sky trembles under too much magnification.

For three days after the accident, she laid unconscious. As he sat for hours beside her, he had to convince himself that she was merely asleep and would soon wake up and kiss him. The same soft breathing that lulled him in the middle of every night lulled him there in the harshness of the hospital room, stroking her hand, whispering to her.

He adjusts the zoom. Through the lens, he can see the number on the wing and just below an open door in the fuselage. He knew when they had children he would be the overcautious one, painting his own dark shadow where she saw only a sunny path to follow. "I have to do this," she explained and for once he had known better than to argue.

Dressed in red, she's no larger than a figurine, white face and white hands as delicate as porcelain. She stands there for a moment, taking in the whole world through her eyes, and then he sees her spread her arms and she's gone, falling as fast as a sack of lead.

That evening he takes her out for a full course dinner at Highland's. She drinks too much champagne, holds on to him across the parking lot. She's asleep before she hits the pillow, and he tucks her into his grandmother's quilt, the one where angels fly.

She wants him to see a doctor about his insomnia, but he knows exactly which part of his mind resists that plunge into the abyss. He climbs out on the gentle part of the roof above the porch and lies there under the stars, counting blazing trails of the meteor shower forecast on the news.

Back in bed he wraps around his wife and closes his eyes. It's the first dream in months he can remember. The inside of the plane is cavernous. He's the only passenger traveling through this night. Standing at the yawning door, he looks out at the velvet curve of the earth, asleep under all those familiar constellations. He knows this time he must jump—and why. He falls through space more like a feather than a man, and there's no parachute in this dream to fail, and he needs none.

SWAN DIVE

The pool shimmers in the morning breeze. She has no towel, no book, no bottle of cream to protect her from the sun. Here at the shallow end a Luna moth as big as her hand floats in one corner, each of its swallowtailed wings marked with a beautiful bullseye.

The words of the preacher keep coming back—"ashes to ashes, dust to dust." The last time she visited Granny Jane the old woman confessed she had never been swimming. In her great-grandmother's time and place, only boys could shed their modesty, only males could plunge themselves into that suspect element. "Baths and baptisms excepted," Granny Jane had laughed.

She herself has lived enough to know that life is matter of drying up. Each of us is born an oasis and gradually lost to the sand. Standing alone in this bright sun, she wonders why she has stayed without a man. Through three engagements she kept believing, only to break things off each time when the magic hour came too near.

Now that 40 is in sight she feels the flow of time quickening, the once wide banks on either side drawing closer, narrowing to a canyon she is about to enter. Granny Jane lived so long they could have fit her shrunken body inside a child's casket.

As a girl she loved to visit the farmhouse on its bluff above the river. She remembers the taste of well water, the fried chickens from Granny's yard, and laying on the feather bed, listening to the black night just outside the open windows.

She would always make a show, rubbing it in. The clumsy boys who were her cousins could manage only belly flops and cannonballs. But she pranced on that barn plank nailed to the dock, the city girl already in gymnastics class, the little ballerina from Birmingham. Up on the bluff she knew Granny Jane was watching.

The breeze dies. The water in the pool is a mirror in which the future is foretold. She knows she will make it to the top of her profession, breaking through the glass ceiling by the force of her own will. She walks to the deep end.

Once in New York she watched a woman stand on a ledge high above the crowded street. The co-workers begging at the window, the police psychologist on his bullhorn—nothing could make her come back inside. The woman fell gracefully, as though she'd once been a diver, plummeting into the giant pillow the rescue squad had inflated below.

Her mind is wandering as she steps on to the board—her Granny's funeral, Fourth of July, the wealthy man still asleep in his house across the lawn. But form is impossible to lose. She takes three steps in her approach, raises one leg and her arms, gets the bounce that will set her free.

Her own weight lifts her, sends her toward an apogee. Toes together, back perfectly arched, she opens more than her arms for that embrace…full of herself, Granny used to say, and falling, falling toward the water.

SABBATH

The surgeon hasn't cut his grass in 15 years. A narrow trail winds through elder thickets higher than our heads. We soon lose sight of the big brick house, but the surgeon's wearing his beeper.

"The fellow before me used to spend every Sunday on his John Deere before he retired and moved into Birmingham. It took him all day to keep this many acres looking like a golf course. And there wasn't one dandelion."

Purple galaxies of ripe berries wheel above us. The surgeon fills his pail with fruit. He says he comes from Illinois where a single field of corn can cover the world. Our trail burrows into tall bamboo that makes a sound like falling rain.

"There's the time the government paid my father not to plant. They called it 'soil banking'. That farmer could hardly stand the sight of precious land pushing up such healthy weeds. But for me it was salvation."

I follow the surgeon through a land of plenty, an uncultivated Canaan where he knows the name and purpose of every living thing. We kneel a dozen different times in 30 feet—Jerusalem artichoke, purple coneflower, soapwort and sumac. On each occasion we behold another gift from nature—food, medicine, clothing, tools. The surgeon gathers his supper as we go, wants me to try his blackberry wine. First, he says, he has a special place to show me.

The trail dips down to a cattail swamp where a pond once sheltered bass and bream. Dynamite under the dam lets the creek meander through a boggy paradise that smells of skunk. But, he says, beavers have just moved in. Soon the water will rise again. He laughs and shrugs.

The one-room cabin stands in a flowery meadow dancing with butterflies. Inside there's a cot, a table, and a kerosene lantern. The work of life and death takes its toll on a man, the surgeon confides. Out here on a Saturday night, on the rarest weekend when he's not on call, he sometimes falls asleep and lets the Sabbath wake him gently, sun in his eyes.

ARCHER

A hundred yards across the field, a black and white circle—a bull's-eye. In the target he sees galaxies collapsing, things so dense and terrible they give away no light.

The anniversary feast he made last night fed only demons as candles danced from shouts and hands struck hard against the table. She did not even try the caviar.

He threw it all in the dumpster—silver, dishes, wine from Bordeaux, wrapped in the heirloom tablecloth. He knew this time she wasn't coming back.

He takes his T-shirt off. The June sun sets the air on fire above the grass. He straps the arm guard on and slips his shooting fingers through the leather tab. His friends had tried to warn him not to soar into the flame again. "I've never known a man like you," she told him the first week they met. One month later he proposed.

With all his strength he bends the bow and strings it. It keeps the shape of gulls above a windy sea. She believes the universe is running down, that life is made of lucky accidents like winning a toy at the fair. He pulls back and releases, feels the note move through his arm and into his chest.

She told him once she spent a summer with her country cousins who poached deer. Riding along with them one night she watched through the bug-spattered windshield as a doe stepped from the pines into their spotlight. "It couldn't move," she said. "Its eyes were big and burning like a thing possessed. They shot it through the heart."

He lays his arrows on the grass and remembers the camp counselor shouting as the other children scrambled to take cover. His first time with a bow, and he'd shot straight up at the sun. Standing there in the wide open his face turned toward the blinding sky, that boy was sure his arrow was never falling back to earth.

"How can you believe in me the way you do?" she asked. "How do you know I won't hurt you too?"

All the arrows at his feet are made for shooting targets except the last one—its metal shaft and bladed razor head are meant for piercing flesh and bone. He slides it on the bow. "Let me go," she said, and he had stepped aside.

Out in the street he watched her taillights disappear, the last two stars in the heavens. He draws the string so hard he feels something must break. Raising up, he aims at the sun, then swings around to the moon rising, the face of hope suddenly blurred by tears. But when he levels off and opens his hand not love but truth drives the shot into that unseeing eye.

DRAGON

She leaves her mother looking at the sonogram, the echo of the fetus like a curving storm on weather radar. She is the only child still to not have children, the gravest sin in her Chinese family. Back home in Birmingham for the first time in years, she marvels at the roots of her own history, the elm trees in the yard so much bigger, her father's garden taking up the whole yard now. She stares up at the mountain.

Her easel is still in the basement. She wipes the dust off one blank canvas, but the paints are dry as stone. At the art store she also buys some brushes; she feels bewildered by the bright rows of paraphernalia, but there's a thrilling flutter in her chest just above the baby.

She drives to the park on the neighboring ridge, the easel anchored in the March dandelions, her long black hair freed from its bun. Just a film of green hangs on the slope across the valley. The twists and turns of the earth are still visible, the cut of muscle and bone. She prepares the brushes and the paints.

She thinks of the elderly Mandarin with a beard like white Spanish moss, called in from Atlanta by her father before he had closed on the house she can see on its concrete street below. Her father said the man practiced *feng shui*. "He is going make sure our home is harmonized with the earth."

Even at that early age she warred with herself, her heart wanting to trust her father's wisdom but her mind needing to make sense. When her father had left the room where the old man stared out the picture window, she marched up to him and questions began tumbling out of her mouth.

"Your family will prosper here because of the dragon," was the only thing he said, his teeth when he smiled the shade of strong tea. He turned and pointed out the window with a finger like a chicken bone.

She remembers how hard she looked—the thick forest on the slope, still bare except for magenta clouds of redbuds blooming, and further up, the gray rocks, a cliff, and a hawk that soared in wide imperfect circles. Suddenly she knew the old man was a fake.

Her teenage years had been rebellious ones. "More American than these Americans," was her father's poor attempt at ridicule. Gifted in art, she had cut her hair short, dyed it, and worn only black, fancying herself the reincarnation of Van Gogh.

Standing in this sunny future, she laughs and wonders what that angry girl would think if she knew her destiny lay in particle physics and a married life without time. For a moment, hand on her stomach, she ponders the child she will soon bear.

Lifting her brush, she is amazed at what she sees, present and past, the universe turning around on itself like a question that is its own answer. Then she begins to paint a mountain but there's a dragon when she's finished.

RED MOUNTAIN CUT

The Red Mountain Cut is a 210-foot-deep, 1,640-foot-long highway cut created through Red Mountain for the Red Mountain expressway into downtown Birmingham, Alabama, a city built to smelt iron ore.

I have come here for perspective. I carry a pack filled with geology texts and a book on Native American customs. I have treatises on Silurian paleontology, magnetic anomalies, and the industrial history of the city. I leave it all by the Red Mountain Museum and walk down the steps into a cold wind above thundering traffic.

The concrete way into the Cut channels a shallow ooze of water the color of blood. I stoop to dip my finger, then draw a vermilion line on the back of my hand.

Creek hunters carried small round containers of magic pigment called red ocher, powdered hematite ore collected from this place where our city sprouted. During the hunt they would use the ocher to paint a forked design beside each eye. The Creeks believed this would let them see as clearly as the peregrine falcon, whose markings they had in mind. Falcons once nested in these heights. Perhaps they will again, soon to be transplanted to downtown towers rising over my shoulder.

The museum staff has placed signs on the rock face describing oceans and mountains that have come and gone, unimaginable time measured in hundreds of millions of years. Layers of sea bottom, thrust up at an angle of force with which the African continent collided with our own, slant above my head. I walk through aeons until I reach the thick iron seams I seek, rusted red by oxygen and rain.

I hold a Boy Scout compass in my hand. Its delicate needle shakes wildly, the guidance it was meant to give thrown off by the chilled flesh on which it temporarily rests. Perhaps there is more, a magnetic flux caused by this much ore, or a pocket of lodestone beneath the mansions on the ridge.

How many commuters in the rush hour below think to look up and wonder? How many know about the core of molten iron that drives the heart of our planet, spinning out invisible threads on which the geese ride? I have proof in my backpack of more amazing things, of iron particles in bacteria lining up toward the poles, of magnetic materials in the belly stripes of honeybees, in the brains of homing pigeons, and the sinus cavities of dolphins. There is speculation even we humans have some similar mechanism beckoning us in unknown ways.

The sleet begins. I run back to my car. I drive down the mountain to the faded elegance of my apartment, built with fortunes made from steel.

The Cherokee suspended a chunk of hematite from a length of string. Muttering incantations, they let their plummet swing, believing it would guide them to what they had lost. On my desk, among the bills and unfinished poems, I leave the compass, its steady finger pointing true.

RAIN DANCE

His first wife would have made him wear galoshes; his second wife would not have noticed the rain. Shoeless he splashes through backyard puddles and thinks of the lover who taught him to walk barefoot ... so long ago, age giving him a soaring eagle's sight.

The beating rain against the umbrella is a symphony of drums. Inside on TV, the talk show has a flash flood warning at the bottom of the screen, a map of Alabama with half its counties colored blue. He stops to check his heart, two fingers on the neck, his racing pulse a signal to the universe of what he is about to do.

He remembers all the buckets on his mother's porch filled with rain. That was a house of women who washed their hair in water from heaven. His own house is empty now except for him—wives, daughters, cats and dogs all departed. He kneels at the gushing downspout outside the bedroom window, cups his hand and drinks.

The pain in his chest has finally left. Standing under the eave, he closes the umbrella and unbuttons his shirt. A few years ago, there would have been a raspberry scar from neck to navel.

They went in with a tube as slim and hungry as a tapeworm, snaking through the bloody river to his heart. Free from obstructions his arteries feed the desire to dance to his legs. The clouds burst once again with distant thunder and he finds himself inside the magic cave in back of the waterfall.

Were he young now he might insist on ballet instead of football, trying out for the School of Fine Arts rather than the line of scrimmage. Five sisters used their only brother as a partner. Arm in arm they led him around the parlor, dipping, swaying, spinning him around the axis of their feminine world until he knew every move.

He thinks how he's been dancing someone else's dance ever since. The rain is coming down so hard he waits behind a liquid curtain made of mercury. He hasn't yet removed the plastic bracelet from the hospital. Reading his name aloud to the waiting rain, he bows forward until his hair is drenched.

Not so long ago he feared his life was over. Unbuckling his belt, he steps out of the past. He looks one last time at the pile of clothes lying at his bare, bony feet, then moves ahead.

The hard rain stings his skin, makes him gasp and laugh. What should he do, he wonders, now that this moment has arrived? And only a few seconds pass, soaking wet, until a rhythm comes up through him, a rhythm entirely his own, and he begins to buck and prance and reel across the lawn toward the willow tree.

—The End—

After graduating from Wabash College, where he studied with the poet, Bert Stern, **Steve Brammell** was supposed to go to graduate school but set off instead on a somewhat picaresque adventure lasting decades. Driven by curiosity, appetite, pride, perfectionism, noblesse oblige, an intermittent mystical affliction, and a distrust of authority, he lived in Europe, the Middle East, North Africa, Austin, Texas, where he was a member of the Austin Poets Theater, Yellow Springs, Ohio, and Birmingham, Alabama, before returning to his beloved Indiana Dunes.

He was gainfully employed at various times as a social worker, teacher, bus driver, patient services coordinator, carpenter, book binder, and gardener, among other jobs, before making his living as a freelance writer for a variety of companies and medical institutions. He also wrote for Alabama Magazine and Birmingham Magazine, in which his monthly feature, The Natural City, looked at local life through a poet's eyes.

A life-time passion for food and wine eventually led him into a parallel career in the culinary world where he helped open three fine-dining restaurants. His prized role was that of wine director, utilizing his extensive experience traveling, visiting wineries and restaurants around the globe, and his own gardening and love of cooking, to provide staff and customers with a sophisticated, yet approachable (and fun), take on gastronomy. He currently is employed in the wine trade in Indianapolis.

His upbringing in rural Indiana gave him a reverence for nature. His father taught him the name of every plant and animal and how to read the lay of the land, as well as the importance of history and science in understanding this world. His mother taught him how to pray and be kind to animals.

He had the good fortune to meet and interact with great writers through the years—James Wright, Robert Bly, Alan Ginsberg, Charles Simic, Etheridge Knight,WS Merwin, Gerald Stern, Eudora Welty, James Dickey, Ann Beattie, Kurt Vonnegut, and many others.

His recent poems and short fiction have appeared in journals such as *RavensPerch, Northwest Indiana Literary Journal, White Wall Review, The Tiny Seed Literary Journal, The Write Launch, Flying Island Journal, Cathexis Northwest Press, Toho Journal* and *The Dead Mule School of Southern Literature.*

He lives in Indianapolis with his wife, who is a nurse. He is a member of the Indiana Writers Center.

CPSIA information can be obtained
at www.ICGtesting.com
Printed in the USA
BVHW030333040321
R11945700001B/R119457PG601494BVX00003B/2